Katie Saves
Thanksgiving

by Fran Manushkin
illustrated by Tammie Lyon

PICTURE WINDOW BOOKS
a capstone imprint

Katie Woo is published by Picture Window Books,
151 Good Counsel Drive, P.O. Box 669
Mankato, Minnesota, MN 56002
www.capstonepub.com

Text © 2011 Fran Manushkin
Illustrations © 2011 Picture Window Books

Printed in the United States of America in Stevens Point, Wisconsin
032010
005741WZF10

Library of Congress Cataloging-in-Publication Data is
available on the Library of Congress website.
ISBN: 978-1-4048-5988-3 (library binding)
ISBN: 978-1-4048-6367-5 (paperback)

Summary: When the Woos' oven quits working,
Katie comes up with a plan to save Thanksgiving.

Art Director: Kay Fraser
Graphic Designer: Emily Harris

Photo Credits
Fran Manushkin, pg. 26
Tammie Lyon, pg. 26

Table of Contents

Chapter 1
Katie Knows Pilgrims

It was Thanksgiving Day. Snow was falling. Lots and lots of snow.

"I can't wait for JoJo and Pedro to come over," said Katie. "This will be our first Thanksgiving together."

"I know a
lot about the
Pilgrims," Katie
told her dad.

"Tell me about them,"
he said.

"It took a long time for
the Pilgrims to cross the sea,"
said Katie. "And their ship,
the *Mayflower*, went through
scary storms."

"JoJo and her family

are driving through a

snowstorm," said Katie.

"I hope they don't get lost."

Chapter 2

Thanksgiving Trouble

"Oh no!" said Katie's

mom. "The stove isn't

working!"

Katie's dad tried to fix it,

but he couldn't.

"The Pilgrims had to eat cold food on the *Mayflower*," said Katie. "Their ship was made of wood. It could burn if they lit a fire."

"Maybe Pedro's family can bring some hot food," said Katie's mom.

She called them, but nobody was home.

"They must be on their way here," said Katie.

"I'll call JoJo," Katie said.

JoJo answered right away.

"Guess what?" said JoJo.

"Our car is stuck in the

snow! We're waiting for a

tow truck."

"This is some
Thanksgiving!"
said Katie's dad
when he heard the news.

"Without the stove, we cannot have sweet potatoes," said Katie's mom.

"Or pumpkin pie," her dad groaned.

Chapter 3
Thankful for Friends

"The snow is piling up,"

said Katie's dad. "I'd better

go shovel it."

"I'll help you," said Katie.

Katie and her dad began

to shovel.

"Mrs. West lives alone,"

said Katie. "I'll shovel her

sidewalk for her."

After a while, Mrs. West
called out, "Katie, thank you
for your help. Come inside.
I made some hot cocoa."

Mrs. West's kitchen was filled with wonderful smells. "I made Thanksgiving dinner for my family," she said.

Just then her
phone rang.
As Mrs. West
listened, her face
grew sadder and sadder.

She told Katie, "My family was going to take an airplane here. But it's a bad day for flying. I guess I will be eating all alone."

Katie looked out the

window. She saw JoJo and

Pedro.

Katie said, "Mrs. West,

why don't you come over

and eat with us?"

"What a wonderful idea!"

said Mrs. West.

"Um," said Katie, "could

you bring your turkey and

sweet potatoes? Our stove

isn't working."

"I would love to!" said

Mrs. West.

Katie and JoJo and Pedro

helped Mrs. West carry the

food to Katie's house.

"This is like the first Thanksgiving," said Katie. "The Pilgrims and the Indians shared their food, too."

"But they didn't have my pumpkin pie," said Mrs. West.

"But WE do!" said Katie.

Everyone was very thankful!

About the Author

Fran Manushkin is the author of many popular picture books, including *How Mama Brought the Spring; Baby, Come Out!; Latkes and Applesauce: A Hanukkah Story;* and *The Tushy Book.* There is a real Katie Woo — she's Fran's great-niece — but she never gets in half the trouble of the Katie Woo in the books. Fran writes on her beloved Mac computer in New York City, without the help of her two naughty cats, Cookie and Goldy.

About the Illustrator

Tammie Lyon began her love for drawing at a young age while sitting at the kitchen table with her dad. She continued her love of art and eventually attended the Columbus College of Art and Design, where she earned a bachelors degree in fine art. After a brief career as a professional ballet dancer, she decided to devote herself full time to illustration. Today she lives with her husband, Lee, in Cincinnati, Ohio. Her dogs, Gus and Dudley, keep her company as she works in her studio.

Glossary

groaned (GROHND)—made a long, low sound to show unhappiness

Mayflower (MAY-flou-ur)—the ship the Pilgrims took when they came to America from England in 1620

Pilgrims (PIL-gruhms)—the group of people who left England, came to America, and formed Plymouth Colony in 1620

sweet potatoes (SWEET puh-TAY-tohs)—thick, sweet, orange vegetables that grow as roots on a viney plant

Thanksgiving Day (thangks-GIV-ing DAY)—an American holiday on the fourth Thursday in November. It remembers the Pilgrims' first harvest feast held in 1621. People give thanks and have a feast on this day.

Discussion Questions

1. The title of this book is *Katie Saves Thanksgiving.* How did she save the holiday for her friends?

2. How do you think Mrs. West felt after she got off the phone with her family? How do you think she felt after Katie invited her over?

3. What are some of your family's traditions at Thanksgiving? Do you watch football? Play games? Enjoy any special recipes?

Writing Prompts

1. Write down three facts you know about Thanksgiving. If you can't think of three, ask a grown-up to help you find some in a book or on the computer.

2. Write a list of five things you are thankful for.

3. Thanksgiving is known for the feasts people make to eat. If you made a Thanksgiving feast, what would you serve? Make a list of all the foods you would make.

Cooking with Katie

In this book, Katie told her dad all about the Pilgrims. The Pilgrims lived back in the 1600s. They wore different clothes than we wear today. For example, the men wore tall black hats with wide brims and square buckles.

With this recipe, you can make a small Pilgrim hat that you can actually eat! Ask a grown-up for permission, and be sure to wash your hands before you start.

Pilgrim Pride Cookies
*Makes 24 cookies

Ingredients:

- 24 shortbread striped cookies
- 12-ounce bag of chocolate chips
- 24 marshmallows
- a tube of yellow decorator's frosting

Other things you need:

- a cookie tray covered with waxed paper
- a medium microwave-safe bowl
- toothpicks

What you do:

1. Set the cookies with the striped-side down on the cookie tray. Space them apart.

3. Pour the chocolate chips in the bowl. Microwave for 1 minute. Stir. If the chips are not all melted, microwave an additional 30 seconds. Stir. Repeat until melted completely.

4. For each one, stick a toothpick into a marshmallow, dip it into the melted chocolate, and then center it on top of a cookie.

5. With a second toothpick, lightly hold down the marshmallow. Carefully pull out the first toothpick.

6. Chill until the chocolate sets. Then use the decorator's frosting to add a small rectangle on the marshmallow near where it meets the cookie. It should look like the gold buckles on Pilgrims' hats.

Everyone will be thankful if you make these tasty treats for your Thanksgiving feast!

WAIT!

Don't close the book!
There's more!

- Learn more about Katie and her friends

- Find a Katie Woo color sheet, scrapbook, and stationery

- Discover more Katie Woo books

All at . . .

www.capstonekids.com

Still want more?

Find cool websites and more books like this one at www.FACTHOUND.com.

Just type in the **BOOK ID**: 9781404859883 and you're ready to go!